Meet Silvermist

By Celeste Sisler

LITTLE, BROWN AND COMPANY
New York • Boston

Attention, Disney Fairies fans!
Look for these words when you read
this book. Can you spot them all?

dress

frog

hat

boots

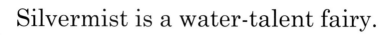

Silvermist is a water-talent fairy.

Her blue dress and pink
flowers are so pretty.

Silvermist lives inside
a drop of water.

She plays dress-up
with a frog in her room.
First, she puts on
a blue ball gown.

Next, Silvermist dresses up

as a pirate fairy.

She has an idea!

Silvermist flies fast
to Tinker Bell's room.
She tells Tink she will have
a pirate party today.

Tinker Bell thinks this is a good idea.

She helps Silvermist get ready

and puts on her pirate outfit.

The two fairies go to Zarina's room.

Zarina jumps with joy!

She will help with the party, too.

Each fairy's pirate outfit includes
a hat, a belt, a pair of boots,
and a hatpin for a sword.

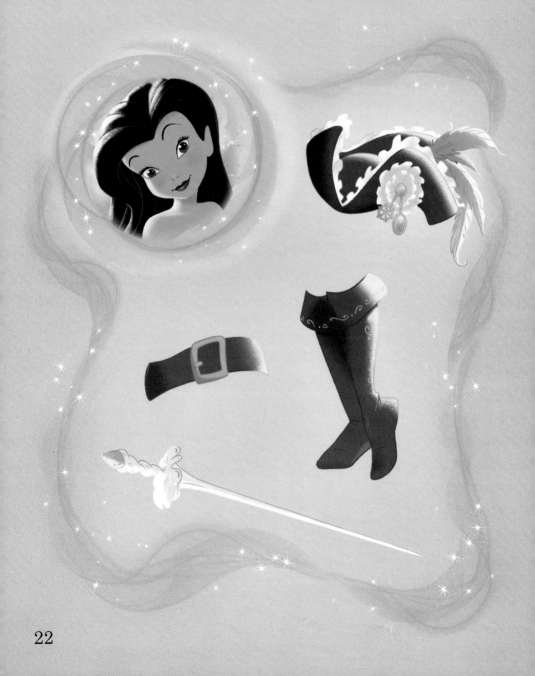

The three fairies fly to a pirate ship.

The other fairies meet them there.

Vidia, Iridessa, Fawn, and Rosetta
are in their pirate outfits.

Baby Crocodile is there, too!

When it is dark out,
the fairies go below the deck
and play games.

The next morning,
Silvermist brings her friends
to a waterfall.

She thanks them
for coming to her party.
She is so happy.

Her fairy friends are happy, too.
Silvermist made their day
bright and fun!